MISSING!

Flame

Have you seen this kitten?

Flame is a magic kitten of royal blood, missing from his own world.
His uncle, Ebony, is very keen that he is found quickly.
Flame may be hard to spot as he often appears in a
variety of fluffy kitten colours but you can recognize him
by his big emerald eyes and whiskers that crackle with magic!

He is believed to be looking for a young friend to take care of him.

Could it be you?

If you find this very special kitten please let Ebony,
ruler of the Lion Throne, know.

Sue Bentley's books for children often include animals or fairies. She lives in Northampton and enjoys reading, going to the cinema, and sitting watching the frogs and newts in her garden pond. If she hadn't been a writer she would probably have been a skydiver or brain surgeon. The main reason she writes is that she can drink pots and pots of tea while she's typing. She has met and owned many cats and each one has brought a special sort of magic to her life.

Magic Kitten

A Very Special Friend

SUE BENTLEY

Illustrated by Angela Swan

PUFFIN

To kittens and puppies everywhere – you're all magic

PUFFIN BOOKS

Published by the Penguin Group
Penguin Books Ltd, 80 Strand, London WC2R ORL, England
Penguin Group (USA) Inc., 375 Hudson Street, New York, New York 10014, USA
Penguin Group (Canada), 90 Eglinton Avenue East, Suite 700, Toronto, Ontario, Canada M4P 2Y3
(a division of Pearson Penguin Canada Inc.)
Penguin Ireland, 25 St Stephen's Green, Dublin 2, Ireland (a division of Penguin Books Ltd)
Penguin Group (Australia), 250 Camberwell Road, Camberwell, Victoria 3124, Australia
(a division of Pearson Australia Group Pty Ltd)
Penguin Books India Pvt Ltd, 11 Community Centre, Panchsheel Park, New Delhi – 110 017, India
Penguin Group (NZ), 67 Apollo Drive, Rosedale, North Shore 0632, New Zealand
(a division of Pearson New Zealand Ltd)
Penguin Books (South Africa) (Pty) Ltd, 24 Sturdee Avenue, Rosebank,
Johannesburg 2196, South Africa

Penguin Books Ltd, Registered Offices: 80 Strand, London WC2R ORL, England

puffinbooks.com

First published 2008
1

Text copyright © Sue Bentley, 2008
Illustrations copyright © Angela Swan, 2008
All rights reserved

The moral right of the author and illustrator has been asserted

Set in Bembo
Typeset by Palimpsest Book Production Limited, Grangemouth, Stirlingshire
Made and printed in England by Clays Ltd, St Ives plc

British Library Cataloguing in Publication Data
A CIP catalogue record for this book is available from the British Library

ISBN: 978-0-141-32354-1

Prologue

The young white lion's heart beat fast as he climbed the dusty hillside. Below him, the valley was shimmering in the heat. All was quiet. Flame felt a surge of hope. Perhaps it was safe to be here.

Suddenly a terrifying roar rang out and an enormous black adult lion bounded on to a rock high above him.

'Ebony!' Flame gasped in fear.

There was a bright flash and a shower

of silver sparks. In the young white lion's place now crouched a fluffy black and white kitten with a bushy tail.

Flame's tiny kitten heart pounded as he backed up slowly and scrambled into a nearby cave. He hoped his disguise would protect him from his uncle.

Flame could hear breathing and there came the sound of claws scrabbling on stone. A huge paw, as big as Flame was now, reached out and scooped him up.

Flame whimpered and tried to struggle free. This was it! The end. But instead of being dragged out on to the hillside he found himself drawn deeper into the cave.

'Greetings, Prince Flame!' rumbled a deep, gentle voice. 'I am glad to see you safe and well. But you have returned at a dangerous time.'

Flame blinked up at the old grey lion with relief. 'Cirrus! I see that my uncle still rules my kingdom.'

Cirrus nodded gravely. 'He does. And he has many spies looking for you. If Ebony finds you, there will be no one to stop his evil.'

'One day I will challenge him and take back the Lion Throne,' Flame mewed bravely, his emerald eyes smouldering.

Cirrus nodded, his worn teeth showing in a proud smile. 'But for now, you must leave. Use this disguise to hide in the other world. Return when you are strong and wise.'

Another fierce roar split the air. Flame

glimpsed a huge dark shape at the cave's entrance.

'Come out, Flame! Let us end this now!' Ebony growled coldly.

'Go! Save yourself!' Cirrus urged.

The tiny kitten mewed as he felt the power building inside him. Silver sparks ignited in his fluffy black and white fur. Flame felt himself falling. Falling . . .

Chapter
★ ONE ★

'Bye! Have a great time. I'll see you both when you get back!' Maddy Briar called, waving to her friends as they walked away from her across the park. Her heart sank as she realized how lonely she now felt. 'Bye. Thanks for nothing,' she grumbled to herself.

Maddy sat on a bench near a big chestnut tree. Kids were zooming up and down the nearby ramps on rollerblades and skateboards. She was itching to join in, but it was going to be weeks before she could do anything but hobble about.

'What a dumb time to break my leg. Right at the start of the summer holidays,' she sighed.

'I got extra large scoops!' Maddy's mum called cheerfully as she came across the grass holding two ice creams. As Mrs Briar saw Maddy's face, she frowned. 'What's wrong?'

'Becky and Lisa are only going away on holiday together with Becky's family. And they didn't invite *me*. They're supposed to be my best friends!' Maddy said crossly.

'I'm sure they still are,' her mum said reasonably. 'They probably didn't think you'd want to go with your broken leg.'

'Huh! They could still have asked me!
I'd have loved to go to Center Parcs, even
if I did have to limp around on crutches,
wearing this zonking great thing!' Maddy
glanced down at the cast, which she'd
decorated with multicoloured felt-tip
drawings and doodles.

'It's not the end of the world, love.
There'll be plenty of other times to go
on holiday with your friends. Budge up,
so I can sit down. Here, take this,' Mrs
Briar held out the ice cream. 'It's starting
to melt.'

'Thanks, Mum,' Maddy said, shifting
up to make room on the bench. 'I'm *so*
bored of sitting about,' she said between
licks.

'Maybe your dad and I can arrange
a few family trips,' Mrs Briar said

thoughtfully. 'At least it's hot enough to wear shorts. We'd have had to cut up your favourite jeans to get them on!'

'And that's supposed to make me feel better?' Maddy murmured gloomily.

It was a beautiful sunny day. The park smelt of cut grass and flowers.

'Where's Dad got to anyway?'

'He's driving Granny Briar to the coach station,' her mum replied. 'She's going to stay with friends for a few weeks. She's a real trooper, isn't she?'

Maddy nodded. Granny Briar had an illness with a long complicated name. It sometimes made her very weak and tired, but that didn't stop her enjoying herself.

'We're keeping an eye on her house and feeding the cats while she's away,' Mrs Briar said.

'I'll help you do that,' Maddy offered. She was fond of her gran's two huge cats, Bradley and Bernie. Perhaps it would also help fill her now empty days. She finished her ice cream. 'What can we do now?'

'I'll bring the car round so you don't have to walk so far and then why don't we go to the museum?' her mum suggested. 'You used to love it in there.'

Maddy's heart sank. 'Yeah! When I was four years old! I'm ten now.'

Mrs Briar stood up. 'Well, you can have a think about it while I get the car. See you in a minute.'

'Humph.' Maddy sat by herself in the sun, swinging her good leg and thinking how unfair everything was. *I bet Becky and Lisa are doing loads of fun things and not going to a boring old museum*, she thought, resting a hand on one of the crutches which were leaning against the bench.

Suddenly there was a dazzling white flash and a shower of silver sparkles from behind a nearby oak tree.

'Oh!' Blinded for a moment, Maddy rubbed her eyes. She looked around. No one else seemed to have noticed what had just happened. Perhaps it had just been the sunlight reflecting off the metal half-pipe on which the skaters were zooming up and down.

Just then a tiny fluffy black and white kitten with a bushy tail crept from behind the tree and came towards Maddy. Its fur seemed to be glimmering with thousands of lights, like miniature fireflies.

'Hello, you. Where did you just come from?' she wondered aloud.

The kitten blinked up at her with the brightest emerald eyes Maddy had ever seen. 'I come from far away. Can you help me?' it mewed.

Chapter
★ TWO ★

Maddy's jaw dropped. She gazed at the kitten in utter astonishment. 'You can talk!' she gasped.

The crutch slipped from her numb fingers. It fell sideways and crashed on to the grass with a loud thud.

'Miaw-ow-ow!' screeched the kitten. It shot into the air on stiff little legs, its hackles raised.

'Sorry. I d-didn't mean to scare you,'

Maddy stammered, reaching down awkwardly.

The kitten's black and white fur all stood on end. Its tail had fluffed right out, but Maddy could see the fear starting to fade from its emerald eyes. 'What is your name?' it asked in a velvety miaow.

'I'm Madeline Briar, but everyone calls me Maddy,' Maddy whispered. She tried to make her voice gentle and friendly, not wanting to frighten away this amazing kitten or attract the attention of anyone else. 'Who are you?'

'I am Prince Flame,' replied the kitten proudly, lifting his pointed chin. 'Heir to the Lion Throne.'

Maddy was having difficulty taking this all in. 'Did you say *Lion* Throne?' she asked doubtfully, looking at his tiny fluffy body.

Flame jumped to the floor and his black and white fur began to sparkle all over. 'Stay back,' he ordered.

Maddy was blinded by another bright silver flash. When she could see again, she saw that the tiny kitten had disappeared. In its place stood a magnificent young white lion, with dazzling velvety fur that gleamed with thousands of diamond-bright lights.

She looked wildly around, expecting people to be running away in fear from the awesome sight. But strangely, everyone was still going about their normal business.

'Do not be afraid, Maddy,' Flame said in a deep rumbling growl.

Then, just as Maddy began to get used to the great white lion, there was a final flash of light and Flame reappeared again as a cute black and white kitten.

'Wow! That's a brilliant disguise,' she whispered. 'No one would ever know that you're a lion prince.'

Flame nodded. 'No one here can see what is happening now, but my disguise will not save me if my uncle finds me. Will you hide me, Maddy? I am in danger!'

Maddy saw that Flame was beginning to tremble with fear. Her heart went out to the tiny kitten. 'Of course I will. But who did you say was after you?'

'My uncle Ebony. He has stolen my throne and sends his spies to find me and kill me,' Flame mewed anxiously.

'Then we have to make sure they never find you. I'll take you home. You can live with me.' Maddy started to bend down to pick Flame up, but in all the excitement she'd forgotten about her leg.

'Oh!' she gasped as she pitched forward.

Maddy braced herself for a painful landing. But she found herself stopping suddenly, frozen in a leaning position. It felt just as if she had bumped gently against an invisible wall.

Time seemed to stand still.

Maddy felt a warm tingling sensation down her spine. Silver sparks ignited in Flame's fluffy black and white fur and his whiskers crackled with electricity. He raised a tiny front paw and a fountain of glittering sparks shot out. They surrounded Maddy, whirling round her like a mini tornado.

She felt herself being set gently on to her feet. The crutches whizzed into the air and then settled themselves under her arms.

Maddy adjusted her balance. She saw that the bright sparks were fading from Flame's fur. He was twitching his bushy tail and looking pleased with himself. 'I hope you are not hurt.'

'No, I'm fine. Thanks, Flame, that was amazing!' Maddy exclaimed.

'I am glad I was able to help,' Flame purred. His furry brow dipped in a puzzled frown. 'Why are you wearing that strange thing on one leg and hopping about on two sticks? Is it a human game?'

Maddy laughed. 'No! I've broken my

leg. This is a plaster cast to keep it straight so it heals properly.' She had a sudden thought. 'Can you use your magic for mending things?'

Flame nodded.

'What . . . like broken legs?' she asked hopefully.

'I could do that, Maddy,' he mewed quietly. 'But how would you explain it without drawing attention to me? That would put me in danger from my enemies. I would have to leave.'

'Oh,' Maddy said, wishing she hadn't asked now. 'I don't want you to have to leave because of me. I reckon I can put up with my broken leg for a bit longer. I'd rather have you for my friend any day. Wait until I tell Mum all about you! She'll be here any minute.'

Flame looked at her seriously. 'You can tell no one about me, Maddy. Will you promise to keep my secret?'

Maddy felt a bit disappointed that she couldn't share her wonderful news, but she was prepared to agree if it helped keep Flame safe.

'OK. Cross my heart and hope to die!' she said. When Flame looked alarmed, she grinned. 'That means yes!'

Flame beamed at her showing just the tips of his tiny sharp teeth. He padded across and twined himself round her ankles. Maddy smiled as his soft fur tickled her bare leg. She already felt fond of the gorgeous kitten and couldn't wait to take him home with her.

'Maddy?' Mrs Briar's voice came floating across the park towards her.

Maddy turned towards her mum with a broad grin. 'Coming!' she called and then smiled down at Flame. Her boring school holiday had just taken a most unexpected turn!

Chapter
★ THREE ★

'I can't believe Mum agreed to let me keep you, just like that!' Maddy said to Flame, patting her duvet for him to jump up beside her. 'I wanted a hamster once and we had a long, boring discussion about why I couldn't have one! Mum must feel sorry for me because of my leg. I'm almost glad I broke it now.'

Flame leapt on to the duvet and began

pedalling it into a cosy nest with his front paws. 'I like it here. This is a safe place,' he purred.

Maddy sat beside Flame, stroking him as he curled into a contented ball. She heard footsteps on the stairs and her dad came into the bedroom.

'You two look cosy!' he said, sitting down and smiling. 'So this is the little chap you found in the park. He's gorgeous, isn't he? What made you call him Flame?'

'He told me that's his na—' Maddy started to answer, then stopped quickly. She was going to have to be a lot more careful about keeping Flame's secret. 'I mean, he just *looked* like a Flame to me,' she said.

'Well, I like it. It suits him.' Mr Briar

stroked one of the kitten's tiny soft ears.
'I'm counting on you to cheer our
Maddy up, Flame. She's been moping
about the house with a long face for
days!'

'I have not!' Maddy said indignantly.
'Well, maybe a bit,' she admitted.

Flame gave an eager little mew and
rubbed his head against her arm.

Mr Briar smiled. 'If I didn't know
better, I'd say that kitten understood every
word.'

Maddy bit back a huge grin. If only
her dad knew!

Throwing back the duvet, Maddy dressed
in shorts and a T-shirt. Flame followed at
her heels as she hobbled downstairs and
went into the kitchen.

Her dad was already in the kitchen, making toast. He looked up and smiled. 'Help yourself to toast, Maddy. Shall I feed Flame to save you bending down?'

'Thanks, Dad,' Maddy said, as her dad forked some tuna into a bowl. He put it down on the floor and Flame began chomping hungrily.

'Your mum's just popped across the road to feed Gran's cats. As soon as she gets back, we're all going out.'

Maddy buttered her toast and took a bite. 'Where are we going?' she asked, munching.

'To Scapley Forest. They've got a brilliant new treetop walk. Your mum picked up a leaflet about it. We thought you might fancy trying it out. It'll cheer you up.'

'Da-ad!' Maddy gave him a pitying look. 'Haven't you forgotten something? My leg!'

Mr Briar rolled his eyes and clapped his hand to his head, pretending that he'd only just remembered. 'Come with me, young lady!'

Puzzled, Maddy got up and hobbled after him. Flame trotted after her curiously.

Her dad opened the porch door. 'There you go!' he said, pointing to the large folded object leaning against the porch wall.

It was Granny Briar's motorized wheelchair. 'Your gran's going through a good patch at the moment, although she took her old manual chair on holiday with her in case she feels poorly. So you could borrow this if you like,' Mr Briar said.

Maddy thought about it. 'It could be fun,' she decided.

Her dad grinned. 'I thought you'd say that! The treetop walk has wheelchair access, so you and Flame will be able to explore it in style.'

Mrs Briar came in the front door. She stepped round Flame and hung Gran's spare house key in the hall cupboard.

'How are Bradley and Bernie?' Maddy asked.

'More enormous than ever. Those cats are spoiled rotten,' her mum replied. 'So, are we all ready to go out?'

Maddy couldn't wait to try the wheelchair. 'You bet!'

★

'This is great fun!' Maddy wheeled along the tree-lined path behind her parents as they followed the signs to the treetop walk. In her lap, Flame lifted his chin, snuffing up the fascinating woodland smells.

The walkway was a series of ramp-like, wooden bridges, which started at ground level. There were special stopping places for wheelchair users. Maddy pulled into one and sat looking out over the fence at the green spreading branches below. Her mum and dad stopped to wait for her.

'Why don't you explore?' Maddy suggested. 'You can leave me to it now. I'll be fine.'

'You do seem to be doing very well. And the walkway's extremely safe. OK,

27

but no messing about,' her dad said,
giving her one of his looks.

'As if!' Maddy said innocently.

'We'll meet you at the observation
tower,' her mum said.

'How cool is this?' Maddy said to
Flame as soon as they were alone. 'It's
dead quiet. Most people must be away on
their holidays.' She took a big breath of
the clean air that somehow tasted so –
green. 'Just looking at these trees and all
this clear blue sky makes you wonder
what it must feel like to fly. It must be
fantastic!'

Flame turned to look at her, his
emerald eyes glinting mischievously.
'Would you like to find out?'

Maddy felt a warm tingling sensation
down her spine as silver sparks ignited in

the kitten's fur and sprayed out of his
whiskers and bushy tail.

'Flame? You wouldn't?' Maddy said
excitedly.

A seat belt appeared from nowhere. It
slid round Maddy's waist and fastened her
in securely. Suddenly the wheelchair
zoomed forward all by itself. Picking up
speed, it headed straight towards a bend
in the walkway.

'We're going too fast to turn,' Maddy
gasped, holding on tight to Flame. Maybe
his magic wasn't strong enough for this.
She screwed her eyes shut. 'Do something,
Flame! We're going to crash!'

Instead of the collision Maddy
expected, there was a sudden silence and
a sensation of lightness. A warm breeze
whizzed past her ears.

'You can open your eyes now, Maddy,' Flame purred.

Very slowly, Maddy opened one eye and then the other. 'Woah!' she gasped, in shock and wonderment. The wheelchair was moving smoothly through the air, metres above the walkway.

They rose higher and higher until they were above the treetops. Scapley Forest and the Northamptonshire countryside were spread out beneath them in a vivid patchwork of velvety greens, deep browns and violet blues.

'What if someone sees us – like Mum and Dad?' Maddy asked worriedly.

Flame grinned up at her. His fluffy black and white fur was ruffled by the breeze. 'I have used my magic to disguise

us. Any humans will see us as a small
cloud.'

A flock of startled-looking Canada
geese flew beneath the wheelchair,
honking in surprise. Maddy waved at
them. Flame's magic spell obviously didn't
work on birds!

'This is like something out of that old
film *E.T.*! I'll never forget this!' she said,
laughing with sheer joy.

Maddy didn't want the amazing magic
journey to end. She could have carried
on floating on for hours, but she knew
her mum and dad would be waiting for
them at the observation tower. They
might come looking if she was away
much longer and she didn't fancy trying
to explain why she and Flame had
disappeared.

'Can you take us back now, Flame?' she asked.

Flame nodded and his whiskers glowed with power. In an instant they were once again floating above the walkway. The wheelchair slowly began to descend. Seconds later, it landed with barely a bump.

'Oh, Flame, that was fantastic!' Maddy said.

Flame rubbed his tiny head against her arm. 'I enjoyed it too!' he mewed happily.

Maddy pressed the controls and with a motorized whirr trundled towards a bend. As she and Flame rounded another bend, the observation tower came into sight. Her parents were still admiring the view. They turned and waved.

'There you are! Come on, slowcoach!

What kept you?' her dad called brightly.

Maddy's eyes met Flame's and they exchanged grins.

You wouldn't believe me if I told you, Dad! Maddy thought.

Chapter
★ FOUR ★

'Here you go, guys!' Maddy said, pouring
cat biscuits into dishes for Bradley and
Bernie.

She was in Granny Briar's kitchen,
helping her mum feed the cats.
Flame had come too. He sat watching
intently as Maddy put the bowls on the
floor. With an eager mew, he leapt
forward and started munching the
biscuits.

'Flame! That's not for you,' Maddy
scolded gently.

Her mum was refilling litter trays. She
looked up and smiled. 'He's all right!
Those two fatties won't miss a few
biscuits!'

Bradley and Bernie gazed placidly at
the tiny kitten as he chomped their food.
Maddy smiled. 'You're right about that.
Oh, well, I don't suppose Flame will need
any supper now,' she said, looking
sideways at the tiny kitten.

It was all she could do not to laugh
out loud, when Flame mewed indignantly.

A few days later, Maddy and Flame sat on
a beach with her parents. A sharp breeze
blew inland and whipped grey clouds
across the sky.

'Whose daft idea was it to have a day trip to the seaside?' Mrs Briar complained.

'You can't please some people!' Mr Briar pulled a face at Maddy as he peeled off his socks and trainers. 'There's nothing like a sea breeze to blow the cobwebs away. I'm going for a paddle. Anyone want to join me?'

'I would but it might get my plaster soggy!' Maddy joked.

Mr Briar laughed. 'I was talking to your mum! But she's got her head stuck in one of her celebrity gossip magazines.'

'I heard that!' Mrs Briar rolled up the magazine and pretended to hit him with it.

Maddy giggled. Sometimes her parents were like a double act!

'Let's go and have a look around,' she

whispered to Flame, struggling to her feet.

Flame nodded eagerly.

'There's a funfair over there. Here you are,' her dad said, seeing her get up. He fished some money out of his jeans pocket. 'This should be enough for some candyfloss and a few goes at trying to win a cuddly toy.'

'Thanks, Dad. Come on, Flame.' Maddy slung her bag over her shoulder and hobbled up the nearby concrete ramp.

Flame scampered after her along the promenade.

The funfair was quite small. It was mostly rides for little kids, but there were a few stalls hung with cheap plastic toys and an arcade with slot machines.

'Let's go into the arcade. The machines might be fun,' Maddy said.

She squeezed awkwardly past two boys who were hanging around the entrance. They looked about twelve years old. One nudged the other and pretended to stick his foot out to trip her up.

'Hey! Watch out!' Maddy warned, almost losing her balance. Flame skittered sideways, narrowly avoiding being kicked.

'Yeah? Or what?' the boy sneered. He had floppy hair and a thin, sharp face.

'Nothing. Just be careful. You almost hurt Flame,' Maddy said, still annoyed.

'Are you giving me orders?' the boy asked.

'N-no.' Maddy's heart started thumping. The boy looked quite tough. She tried to back away, but it was difficult to move quickly on crutches.

'Leave it, Ed,' the other boy said. 'She isn't doing anything.'

Ed's thin face darkened. 'Who asked you? I'm not having some nerdy girl bossing me about!' He swooped down and lifted Flame up by the scruff of his neck. 'I've just lost a kitten and this one looks just like it. I'm taking it home with me.'

Flame gave a howl of protest. His legs and paws were dangling in mid-air and his bushy tail was thrashing helplessly.

'Hey! Give him back. He's mine,' Maddy burst out.

'Make me!' Ed challenged and then he smiled slowly as if he had a better idea. 'Hold on. Maybe I *don't* want the little fleabag!' He swung his arm in an arc and seemed about to fling Flame across the fairground.

Chapter
★ FIVE ★

'No, don't!' Maddy screamed. She dropped
her crutches and lunged towards Ed.

Taken by surprise, the older boy
dropped Flame.

Maddy just managed to catch the
terrified kitten round the middle. Flame
whimpered. His eyes were wide with
panic as he scrabbled for a foothold. His
tiny razor-sharp claws raked Maddy's bare
arms.

Ignoring the pain, Maddy drew Flame close against her T-shirt and wrapped her arms round his trembling body.

Ed still stood there scowling. He looked from Maddy to Flame. Maddy's mouth dried. He was going to try and grab Flame again!

She glared at the older boy, too angry now even to be scared of him. 'Just you try it!' she said through gritted teeth.

Ed's friend nudged him. 'Come on. She's not worth it.'

Ed looked at Maddy's pale, set face. 'Yeah! I'm bored of this. Keep your dumb kitten!'

As Ed and his friend slouched off, Maddy sagged against the doorway. Her legs were shaking and she felt all wobbly inside.

Flame reached up and touched her chin with a tiny front paw. 'Thank you for saving me, Maddy. You were very brave.'

'I wasn't really, but I wasn't going to let that bully hurt you,' Maddy said. She winced at the pain in her clawed arms. Now that the excitement was over they felt really sore.

'You are hurt! Quickly, slip me under your T-shirt,' Flame ordered.

Maddy huddled just inside the arcade with her back to the open doorway. As soon as she covered Flame with her T-shirt, she felt a warm prickling against her skin and heard the faint crackling of sparks. Her sore arms stung sharply for a second and then the pain seemed to drain away. When she looked for the scratch marks, she saw that they had completely disappeared.

She lifted Flame out from under her T-shirt and gave him a cuddle. 'Thanks, Flame. Maybe you should hide or something in case we bump into that mean boy again.'

'Do not worry, Maddy. I will use my magic so that only you can see and hear me.'

'Good idea. If you're invisible, you'll be extra safe.' Maddy slipped Flame into her shoulder bag, where he sat with his paws hooked over the side, looking out. She bent down awkwardly to pick up her crutches.

'Do you need some help?' said a friendly voice.

Maddy straightened up.

She saw a girl with short brown hair and a round face. She wore shorts and a T-shirt with a sparkly red star on it. The girl smiled. 'I'm Chloe,' she said, picking up the crutches and handing them to Maddy. 'How did you break your leg?'

Maddy settled herself back on her crutches. 'Thanks, Chloe. I'm Maddy. I did it when I fell off my rollerblades.'

'That was bad timing, right at the start of the summer hols!' Chloe said sympathetically.

Maddy nodded. 'Tell me about it!'

As she hobbled away from the arcade, Chloe walked beside her. 'I saw those rotten boys picking on you. I hate people who behave like that!'

'Me too! It was pretty horrible for a minute. Especially when he . . .' Maddy tailed off uncertainly. Had Chloe seen Ed grab Flame? Or had she been too far away? Maddy decided not to mention her magical friend. It would be too awkward to try and explain where Flame had suddenly gone. 'Anyway, I'm all right now,' she finished saying.

But Chloe wasn't listening any more. She was staring past Maddy, her eyes widening with astonishment as she gazed at Maddy's shoulder bag.

Maddy was stunned. It was as if Chloe could see Flame hanging over the side of the bag, but she knew that was impossible. Flame was only visible to her.

A cute black Labrador puppy ran out from behind a sweet stall. It had a plump little body, enormous paws and shiny, coal-black fur. His eyes were an unusual bright midnight blue.

Panting, the puppy trotted over and plonked itself at Chloe's feet.

'Oh, isn't he gorgeous! What's his name?' Maddy said delightedly.

Chloe's jaw dropped. 'You can see Storm?'

Maddy took a second look at the cute puppy's enormous bright blue eyes. A memory stirred in her mind. The first time she had seen Flame, she had noticed his amazing emerald eyes. A thought struck her and her tummy fluttered with excitement.

'Is Storm a magic puppy?' she asked Chloe.

Chloe gasped and went bright red. 'I . . . um . . . don't know what you mean.

I have to go . . .' She bent down and
picked up the puppy.

'It's OK. I know about magic animals,'
Maddy said hastily, hoping to stop Chloe
running off. 'I've got one too. Flame's a
magic kitten.'

Chloe looked shocked and then a huge
smile spread across her face. 'I thought he
might be, but I couldn't believe it! This is
amazing! How did you find Flame?'

'Shall we find somewhere quieter
where we can talk?' Maddy suggested.
She couldn't wait to hear all about Storm.

Chapter
★ SIX ★

'Where did you find Fla–'

'Where did you find Sto–'

Both girls began talking at the same time. Maddy grinned. 'You go first!'

'I found Storm hiding in our back garden, behind Dad's shed,' Chloe explained. 'I fell in love with him on the spot.'

Maddy told Chloe about finding Flame in the park. 'Luckily my parents agreed that he could live with me!'

'Mine did too. I don't know what I'd have done if they'd refused,' Chloe said.

Maddy smiled at Chloe, liking her more and more. Maybe they could become good friends, especially as Chloe understood about Flame, and her summer wouldn't be so lonely after all.

Maddy and Chloe were sitting on a cast-iron bench on a quiet stretch of the promenade. There was the sound of waves breaking and cries of the gulls wheeling overhead. Some distance away, the pier stretched out into the sea.

Maddy sat with her bag on her lap. Flame was still inside it and Chloe reached out to stroke him. 'Hi, Flame. It's great to meet you.'

'Greetings, Chloe. I am pleased to meet you,' Flame purred.

Maddy stroked Storm. 'Hi, Storm.'

Storm showed his teeth in a doggy grin. 'I am very pleased to meet you, Maddy,' he woofed.

Maddy waited to see if Flame and Storm would talk to each other. Did they even speak the same language? She realized that they might have actually come from completely different worlds.

Flame's ears flattened as he looked curiously across at Storm.

Storm turned towards the tiny kitten. Lifting his lip, he gave a warning growl.

'Oh, I was hoping that Flame and Storm would like each other,' Maddy said disappointedly.

'Well, I guess cats and dogs *are* natural enemies,' Chloe said.

'But Flame's not a cat as his true self. He's a –' Maddy bit her lip, suddenly remembering that she couldn't say any more. 'Sorry. I've promised to keep Flame's secret from everyone.'

Chloe nodded. 'That's OK. I understand. I've promised to keep Storm's secret too.'

'Shall we move on a bit? Flame and Storm might enjoy a run about on the beach together,' Maddy suggested hopefully.

'Good idea.' Chloe quickly called Storm to heel and the Labrador puppy scampered along beside her for a few metres.

Maddy opened her bag for Flame to jump out, before picking up her crutches.

But as soon as they reached the beach,

Storm gave an excited bark and rushed at
Flame.

Flame tore off across the sand with
Storm hot on his heels.

'Oh, well, playing chase is a start, I
suppose,' Chloe said.

Maddy wasn't so sure.

Storm lolloped about, ears flapping and
big paws churning up sand as he invited
Flame to play. Flame danced sideways,
trying to avoid being buried under the
sand or squashed by the boisterous
pup.

'Gro-oof!' Storm woofed encouragingly.
Skidding right up to Flame he gave him
a friendly nip on the ear.

Flame's emerald eyes flashed with
indignation. Lifting one tiny paw, he
swiped Storm across his moist black nose.

'Ooo-oof?' The puppy stopped dead, a surprised expression on his face.

'Careful, Flame! You could have really hurt Storm!' Chloe cried.

Maddy rushed to Flame's defence. 'He was only sticking up for himself!'

Chloe frowned as she bent down to stroke Storm and check his nose for scratches. 'He seems OK, but I think I'd better go back to my mum and dad now.'

'OK,' Maddy said, trying hard to hide her disappointment. She'd only just found Chloe and now it seemed as if she wasn't going to get to know her at all. 'Why don't we swap phone numbers and addresses first?' she suggested hopefully.

To her relief, Chloe nodded. She produced a small notebook and pen and they scribbled down their details.

When Maddy read Chloe's address, her eyes widened. 'You live in Green's Barton? That's amazing! It's only about twenty minutes by car from Northampton where I live! Why don't we meet up when we get back home?'

Chloe frowned. 'I don't know if it's such a good idea if Flame and Storm don't like each other. Maybe I'll ring you. I'll have to think about it. Come on, Storm,' she called, walking away with the black puppy bounding after her.

Maddy watched them go with a familiar sinking feeling of loneliness. She didn't think that she would hear from Chloe again.

Chapter
★ SEVEN ★

Later that evening, after supper, Maddy
lay stretched out on the sitting-room sofa.
She was trying to cheer herself up by
reading one of her favourite music
magazines. Flame was curled up in her
lap.

'I like Chloe. It will be good to see
her again,' he mewed pointedly. Maddy
noticed that he didn't mention Storm.

'I don't think there's much chance of

that,' Maddy said, stroking his tiny ears.
She loved Flame to bits, but it would
have been brilliant to have another friend
who understood about magical animals.
She let out a long sigh.

Flame looked at her, his furry brow
wrinkling in concern. 'You look sad,
Maddy,' he mewed.

'Yeah. I s'pose I am,' Maddy admitted.
'I really like Chloe and it doesn't help
that she's not bothered about being
friends when I know that she lives so
close. It's a shame that you and Storm
don't get on,' she said sadly.

Flame didn't reply, but he seemed
thoughtful.

Just then Maddy's mum came into the
room. 'Oh, there you are. I've just been
up to put some clean washing in your

bedroom, young lady. It's a complete tip.
Can you go and tidy it, please?'

'Oh, Mu-um. Do I have to do it now?'
Maddy groaned.

'Yes! Off you go,' Mrs Briar said firmly.

Maddy slid off the sofa and stumped
moodily out of the room. Flame followed
as she went upstairs.

Maddy stood looking at all the clothes,
shoes and rubbish lying around. 'Great!
It's going to take me ages to clear all this
up. Just what I need. A rotten job to
finish off a rotten day!'

Flame jumped on to the window sill.
'May I help?'

Maddy felt the special tingling down
her spine, as silver sparks bloomed in
Flame's black and white fur and his
whiskers crackled with electricity.

Phlap! Clothes shot through the air and plonked themselves into the linen basket. Clatter and rustle! Books and shoes tidied themselves into piles and rubbish shot into the waste bin. Whirr-rr and flip! A Hoover and a feather duster appeared out of thin air and zipped about vacuuming and cleaning up.

'Wow! That's amazing!' Maddy clapped her hands in delight. 'Tidying my room's a breeze with you around!'

'You are welcome,' Flame purred. He paused and looked up at her with concerned bright eyes. 'I know that you would like to be friends with Chloe, so I will try to get on with Storm.'

'Aw. That's so sweet of you!' Maddy smiled, feeling a surge of affection for him. 'Thanks, Flame.' She hadn't the heart

to tell him that he probably wouldn't
get the chance to make up with Storm
now.

Leaving Flame curled up on her bed,
Maddy went to the bathroom to brush
her teeth.

When she came back, Flame wasn't on
the bed. Maddy peered underneath but
he wasn't there. She opened her wardrobe
and found Flame tucked into a tight ball
in one corner.

'What's this — hide-and-seek?' she asked
grinning, but then she saw that Flame
was trembling all over.

His emerald eyes were wide and fearful.
'My enemies . . .' he whimpered.

Maddy's chest tightened. 'Are . . . are
they close? You're not leaving *now*, are
you?' she asked, stroking him gently.

Flame shook his head. 'But if they find me I will have to go at once.'

Maddy didn't even want to think about that. 'I hope they'll just go past and then you can stay here forever!'

'One day I must take my rightful place on the Lion Throne. Do you understand that, Maddy?' he mewed seriously.

Maddy nodded, swallowing the lump that rose into her throat. 'But that might not be for ages. I'll just have to be extra careful to keep you hidden.'

Flame's ears flattened and he curled into an even tighter ball.

Chapter
★ EIGHT ★

To Maddy's relief, Flame seemed to be back to his normal self when she woke next morning. He jumped up on to the bed and greeted her with an extra loud purr.

'Have your enemies gone far away?' she asked him.

Flame nodded. 'They have for now. That means I can stay a little longer.'

Maddy picked Flame up and cuddled

him as they went downstairs for breakfast. As she reached the hall the phone rang.

It was Chloe. 'Hi, Maddy. I wondered if it was still OK for me to come over?'

'You bet! I'd love you to!' Maddy said delightedly. 'But what about Storm? He's really not keen on Flame, is he?'

'No, but we've talked about it and he's agreed to try harder to get on with Flame, so it's no problem,' Chloe said.

'Cool! Why don't I ask Mum if you can stay over?'

Chloe agreed readily and it was all arranged. 'See you on Saturday then!' Maddy said, before replacing the phone and grinning.

Maddy was feeling much happier as she helped her mum make up the spare bed for Chloe. 'Your room's very clean and tidy now. I *am* impressed,' Mrs Briar commented.

Maddy winked at Flame.

Chloe and Storm arrived just before Saturday lunchtime. Mrs Briar made them a delicious picnic. There were even packets of kitten and puppy treats. 'It's a lovely day. Why don't you go to the park? It's probably best to be out from under your dad's feet when he's decorating. Besides, Storm and Flame might enjoy some fresh air,' she suggested.

'Good idea, Mum!' Maddy, Chloe, Storm and Flame all trooped off.

After they had finished eating, Maddy watched as Chloe produced a ball and

played a game of 'fetch' with Storm.
Flame remained curled up beside her.

'Sorry I can't run around with you. I'll
have my cast off soon and then I'll make
up for it,' Maddy said apologetically.

'It is no problem,' Flame purred,
yawning. 'I like having lots of naps.'

Twenty minutes later, Chloe came
running over, her cheeks glowing. 'Phew!
I'm worn out now. But Storm never
seems to get tired. He still wants to play,'
she puffed.

Storm trotted over to Flame and
plonked down close to him. He lay with
his head on his paws, keeping a watchful
eye on the kitten. Flame looked sideways
at the black puppy and his tail twitched
from side to side with irritation, but he
stayed put.

'I thought coming to the park was a good idea, but I'm not sure it's made much difference,' Maddy whispered to Chloe. 'Let's go home. I've got a new DVD we can watch.'

'Sounds good,' Chloe said, shaking her head at them both.

Flame came into the bathroom with Maddy when she went to clean her teeth before bed. He jumped up on to the side of the bath and perched there watching her.

There was a bucket of something soaking in the bath. Maddy poked it experimentally. It looked liked the overalls her dad had been wearing for his decorating.

As Maddy was putting her toothbrush

away, the bathroom door opened and Chloe came in. 'Oh, sorry. I didn't know you were still in here.'

'That's OK. I must have forgotten to lock the door,' Maddy said. 'I've finished now anyway. Bathroom's all yours. Come on, Flame.'

Before Maddy could move, Storm shot through Chloe's legs and darted into the room. His eyes glowed mischievously as he saw Flame poised on the edge of the bath. With a playful woof he leapt straight at him.

'No, Storm! There's a buck—' Maddy cried, but it was too late.

As Flame jumped nimbly out of the way, Storm tumbled into the bath and crashed straight into the bucket, tipping it over.

'Yipe! Yipe!' Storm whined in alarm as the wet overalls slopped on to him and he skidded around in their slimy, soapy embrace.

Maddy and Chloe fell about laughing.

'Looks like someone's going to need a bath before bedtime!' Maddy said.

Storm managed to crawl out from under the overalls. He seemed to be enjoying all the fuss. Cocking one ear, he sat with his black fur sticking up in wet spikes.

Chloe knew what bathing Storm would entail. She stopped laughing. 'It's going to take hours. We'll be here till way after midnight!' she groaned.

'Not if we have some help. Flame?' Maddy said meaningfully.

Flame got the message. 'Very well.

I will help,' he mewed, pointing a tiny front paw at Storm.

A big shower of silver sparks shot out and rained gently down on to the soaked puppy. There was a fizz and crackle of power and Storm was clean and dry in a trice; Mr Briar's overalls were once again soaking in their bucket.

'Wow! That was neat! Thanks, Flame,' Chloe said. She picked Storm up and rubbed her chin against his fluffy black fur.

Flame gave her a furry grin. 'You are welcome,' he purred. 'And so is Storm,' he added after a brief pause.

Storm eyed Flame with surprised midnight-blue eyes. He made a sound that was halfway between a whine and a growl. 'Thank you. But I could have used my own magic,' he woofed politely.

'It was still really nice of Flame to help,' Chloe said.

Storm didn't answer. He trotted out of the bathroom with his nose in the air.

Maddy sighed. 'I guess you could call that progress,' she said doubtfully. 'Let's all go to bed.'

The following morning, Maddy's mum was busy at her sewing machine. 'I've promised to have these curtains finished for when your gran gets back. Oh, bother! I've just remembered. I haven't fed her cats yet.'

'We'll go and feed them,' Maddy offered, 'won't we, Chloe?'

Chloe nodded.

'Wait until you see Bradley and Bernie.

They are mega-enormous, like two huge sacks of fur!' she said to Chloe as they wandered over to Gran's house.

'I can't wait to see them,' Chloe said, grinning.

As Maddy unlocked the front door she heard scuffling sounds from the sitting room. 'I hope Bradley and Bernie aren't getting up to mischief in there,' she commented going into the hall. She pushed open the sitting-room door and froze in shock.

Two big men were stuffing a silver tea set and some ornaments into a bag. One of the patio doors was broken and there was glass all over the floor.

Maddy heard Chloe's sharp intake of breath behind her. 'Quick! Let's go and get help!' Chloe whispered.

But it was too late. At that moment one of the men turned round. 'Hey! Where'd those kids come from?'

'Who cares? Grab the stuff and let's get out of here!' the other one cried.

Maddy's pulse raced. Despite her fear, she felt a surge of anger. Before she could think better of it she thrust her crutches away and limped forward. 'You leave my gran's stuff there!' she ordered.

The bigger man laughed. 'What're you going to do if we don't?'

'We'll phone the police and tell them what you look like!' Maddy fumed. 'They probably already know who you are!'

The big man looked at his mate and Maddy knew she'd hit a nerve. The burglars made for the patio door with all her gran's things in their bag.

Time suddenly seemed to stand still. Maddy felt a familiar prickling sensation down her spine as two small shapes, trailing sparks like comets, hurtled into the room past her and Chloe.

Flame's whiskers crackled as he raised a tiny paw and sent a spray of silver glitter whooshing towards the bigger man.

The man stopped dead. He dropped the bag and began marching jerkily on the spot like a rusty clockwork soldier. 'Help! What's happening?' he cried in a panicky voice.

Storm's thick black fur bloomed with gold sparks and his tail fizzed with electricity. He huffed out a big cloud of gold glitter at the other burglar.

The second man started marching clumsily on the spot like his mate. 'This place is haunted. Let me out!' he yelled.

Flame glanced at Storm, his emerald eyes gleaming. Storm gave a gleeful woof. As if at an invisible signal, the kitten and puppy raised their paws at the same time. A shimmering fountain of gold and silver sparks whooshed towards the burglars.

The men swivelled on the spot. With confused expressions, they started doing a jerky monster march towards the patio door and then high-stepped down the garden.

Maddy and Chloe cracked up laughing.

'They look like mad puppets!' Chloe said.

'They're not so tough now. Not with Flame and Storm on their case!' Maddy crowed.

'He-elp!' The burglars' cries grew

fainter as they stamped towards the garden fence. Suddenly the magic seemed to wear off. Still yelling, they scaled the fence and were gone.

The sitting room lit up with a bright flash of silver and gold light. Maddy saw that the patio door had been mended and the silver tea set and ornaments were back in place. 'Thanks, you two,' she said, beaming at Flame and Storm.

'Yeah! You make a brilliant team!' Chloe said. 'I don't think those burglars will be back!'

Flame started purring. He padded over to Storm and rubbed his head against the puppy's shoulder. Storm wagged his tail and began licking the top of Flame's tiny head.

Maddy and Chloe smiled in delight.

A loud wail of complaint came from the doorway – Maddy almost jumped out of her skin. But it was only Bradley and Bernie, telling her they were fed up of waiting for their food!

Chapter
★ NINE ★

'Having a magical friend is the best ever, isn't it?' Chloe said, cuddling Storm.

It was Sunday afternoon and they were sitting in the back garden waiting for Chloe's parents to come and fetch her.

'We're so lucky,' Maddy said, breathing in Flame's sweet kitten smell as she stroked his soft head.

Suddenly, Storm whimpered. Tucking

his tail between his legs, he began
trembling all over.

'What's wrong?' Chloe asked him
worriedly. 'Are you sick?'

Maddy saw two mongrel dogs trotting
down the garden. 'How did they get in
here?'

Chloe paled. 'Storm! Look out!'

As Maddy watched, the dogs instantly
doubled in size and sprouted huge teeth.
Their pale eyes fixed on Storm with a
cold purpose.

Suddenly there was a blinding gold
flash. Storm was no longer a cute black
puppy. He had become a magnificent,
silver-grey wolf cub. A female wolf with
a gentle face stood next to him.

'Save yourself, Storm!' Chloe burst out.

The wolf cub turned to her with

glowing blue eyes. 'Farewell, Chloe. You have been a good friend.'

Storm turned to Flame and bowed his head. Flame returned Storm's bow. 'Good luck, Storm,' he purred softly.

There was another bright flash and gold sparkles rained down on to the lawn around Maddy, Chloe and Flame. Storm and the she-wolf faded and were gone. The mongrels shrank back to normal size and disappeared too.

Maddy stood in silence, stunned by what had just happened.

'I'm really going to miss Storm,' Chloe whispered, her voice breaking.

Maddy threw her arms round Chloe, her heart aching for her friend. 'I'm so sorry that he's gone.'

Chloe nodded tearfully. 'I knew he'd

have to go one day. I'm just glad he's safe. And at least I had a chance to say goodbye.'

Maddy felt a stir of sadness. She remembered that Flame's enemies had already come very close. How much longer was her magical friend going to be able to stay with her?

Chloe didn't phone Maddy for a few days.

Maddy knew that her friend was still upset about losing Storm. Her dad said it was sometimes best to give people space to get over things in their own way, and so she followed his advice.

But Maddy was delighted when Chloe rang her the following week and sounded more like her old self.

'I have to go to hospital to have my plaster off tomorrow,' Maddy told her. 'I can't wait, but I'm a bit nervous about it.'

'I'll come with you!' Chloe offered at once. 'Oh, but you probably won't need me, will you? You've got Flame,' she added uncertainly.

'I know I have, but it'd be great if you came too!' Maddy said. 'I'd love to see you and so would Flame. Afterwards, we can all celebrate having my leg back to normal with a pizza or something.'

'OK then it's a deal!' Chloe said. 'What time do you have to go to the hospital?'

Maddy sat in a long queue in the hospital waiting room. A nearby sign read, *Orthopaedics Outpatients.*

Adults and kids with all kinds of plaster

casts and support collars sat looking
bored. 'We're going to be ages yet,'
Maddy complained to Chloe.

'Why don't you, Chloe and Flame go
for a walk in the grounds? I'll come and
get you when your name's called out.'
Mrs Briar suggested.

Maddy nodded. 'Anything's better than
sitting here.'

In the grounds, they found a quiet
corner with a square pond and a small
stone statue. Maddy put her shoulder bag
down, so that Flame could jump out.

Flame darted in and out of the bushes,
play-growling at a drowsy bumblebee.
Maddy laughed at his antics.

Chloe smiled, a wistful look on her
face. Maddy knew she was thinking of
Storm.

Suddenly Maddy glimpsed fierce shadowy cat shapes peering into the bushes. Her heart missed a beat. But Flame had sensed them.

There was a flash of dazzling bright light. The bushes parted and Flame stepped out: a tiny black and white kitten no longer, but a magnificent young white lion. At his side was an older, adult grey lion.

'Wow!' Chloe gasped, stunned.

Maddy felt a sharp pang as she realized that the moment she had been dreading was here. She rushed forward and threw her arms round Flame's muscular neck. 'Oh, Flame. I'm going to miss you so much!' she cried.

Flame allowed her to hug him for a moment longer and then he stepped back.

'Be well, Maddy. You have been a good friend.'

More silver sparkles crackled in the air and there was a final blazing flash of light. Flame raised a large white paw in farewell and then he and the older lion were gone. There was a terrifying howl of rage from the fierce dark cats, before they too disappeared.

A deep sadness welled up in Maddy. She couldn't believe Flame had had to go so suddenly. She was going to miss him terribly.

'I'll never forget you, Flame,' she whispered as her eyes pricked with tears. She knew she would always treasure the time she had shared with the tiny magic kitten.

Maddy turned to Chloe and the two

girls hugged in complete understanding.

'Maddy!' called Mrs Briar, waving at them from the hospital entrance. 'The nurse just called your name out!'

'Coming!' Maddy called, wiping away her tears. She took a deep breath. 'I'll be *so* glad to get this thing off!'

Linking arms with Chloe, Maddy and her lovely new friend went towards the hospital. Somehow she knew that Flame and Storm were watching over them both and it made her smile.

A Summer Spell
9780141320144

Classroom Chaos
9780141320151

Star Dreams
9780141320168

Double Trouble
9780141320175

Moonlight Mischief
9780141321530

A Circus Wish
9780141321547

Sparkling Steps
9780141321554

A Glittering Gallo
9780141321561

Seaside Mystery
9780141321981

Firelight Friends
9780141321998

A Shimmering Splash
9780141322001

A Puzzle of Paws
9780141322018

A Christmas Surprise
9780141323237

Picture Perfect
9780141323480

A Splash of Fore
9780141323497